Alan Blackwood was a book publishing editor for much of his working life while writing numerous books on music. Now in his later years, he has turned to fiction, but with a big big difference. In his first published set of short stories, *Snap Shots*, Alan aimed for brevity, in the belief that less is more. In *Post Mortem* he has taken the process further, concentrating his thoughts into a gem-like finish. From the erotic to the sad and sometimes darkly humorous, the thoughts, images, and situations have spilled out of him. You can't call them stories. 'Vignettes' is the word that springs to mind. Do they work? Over to you, dear reader.

For Sally

Alan Blackwood

POST MORTEM

AUSTIN MACAULEY PUBLISHERS™

LONDON • CAMBRIDGE • NEW YORK • SHARJAH

A CIP catalogue record for this title is available from the British Library.

ISBN 9781398492202 (Paperback)
ISBN 9781398492219 (ePub e-book)

www.austinmacauley.com

First Published 2023
Austin Macauley Publishers Ltd®
1 Canada Square
Canary Wharf
London
E14 5AA

Table of Contents

POST-MORTEM

SHE jumped from the taxi, ran across the road to her block of flats, fumbled with the entrance keys and fumbled again with the ones to her door, which she closed noiselessly behind her. The neighbours heard everything.

In the bathroom mirror, she inspected the swollen bite on her lip. Dinner with the boss before the naked, grabbing, grinding, trembling climax to what they call the Little Death.

Sober now with the chill first light of another day, she lay on her bed with a plaster on her lip and a part of him still inside her. She slept but not for long. How to face them at work?

BLIND DATE

THE moment she stepped onto my train, it all came flooding back—the dating agency. We arranged to meet at Holborn Station. She'd be wearing a lucky rabbit's foot in her lapel.

She hadn't sounded too bad on the phone, and riding the escalator came a first little stab of arousal. Not for long, not with those two buck teeth settled on her lower lip, giving her—how to describe it—that homely look. Straight back down the other escalator, she'd never know.

Now here she was again, the same two teeth without the lucky rabbit's foot. Susie Rose. How long, I wonder, did she wait at Holborn Station, all of 20 years ago?

Forgive me, Susie, for a second time if you can.

HAPPY DAYS

WHAT game, eh!' He joined me on the seat, a white carnation in his buttonhole and a bottle of bubbly in his hand. 'Like some?'

We sat and watched the merry throng having their pictures taken outside the gothic house in the park. 'Not your wedding, is it?'

He tried a rueful smile. 'Not this time.'

'Terry!' An upright young lady in floral hat and gripping a large shiny black handbag stood a little way off. 'Come on. It's goin' to pour in a minute.'

The sky had turned the colour of a deep bruise, while there came that rare and fleeting fragrance as the first swollen raindrops soaked into the warm, dry ground.

Terry clambered to his feet and crushed out his cigarette.

'What a game, eh!'

13

VIA CRUCIS

A S David was a man of the cloth, I thought he might like
to see the chapel in my favourite cemetery up in the
hills.

Cypresses, grown old on the compost of death, swayed
and sighed to the chill, dry mistral wind. Inside the chapel, the
sudden silence was awesome. A faint light from one small
east window fell like a tear upon the bare white altar and we
breathed in cold stone. Jessica shivered. 'This place gives me
the creeps.'

That left the iron crucifix from the cemetery dump now
hanging on my wall. Jessica drained her wine glass. 'David,
it's time to go.'

She poked her head out of their car window. 'We'll pray
for you,' she cried as the mistral blew them away.

WISHING WELL

IT'S written in stone, as sure as the Ten Commandments. Hope for something, wish for something and it's not going to happen.

So what's not going to happen. She'll phone in a minute in that soft, sweet voice that melts my heart. She'll phone tomorrow. She'll email to ask if she can come round. Okay, she'll look in tomorrow to ask how I'm getting on with work and if there is anything I need. Or she'll ask me to play the piano, her favourite Mendelssohn Song Without Words or the Chopin Waltz or maybe that lovely old standard, It Had To Be You.

It isn't. That's the bloody trouble.

PAPER TIGER

'TIPPOO'S Tiger', the great title for a book, inspired by the exhibit in the Victoria and Albert Museum of such a beast savaging a red-coated soldier.

It had once belonged to the Sultan Tippoo of Mysore, killed fighting the army of the British East India Company, and now the subject of Richard's book. I'd watched him go bald and myopic as he laboured at it.

Up on his wall was an old poster for a production of *King Lear* with his name among the cast. Another member of that cast was now a star of stage and screen. It hadn't happened for Richard, but he did have 'Tippoo's Tiger'.

He reached for my bottle on the floor. 'I mean, what have I got to lose?'

Not his hair, I guess.

GAY ABANDON

GRACE picked up her flute and played the opening phrase of Francis Poulenc's sonata for that instrument, music so elegant, so wistful, so totally French. With Cynthia on the piano, living together, pushing a certain age but probably still up for it, one way or the other.

More music, more wine, and I daren't drive home, a threesome. Oh boy! Shoes off and onto the bed, not in it, me in the middle. Lights out. Crash.

Through the curtains, a cold fuzz of daylight, the hangover not yet descended, black coffee, eyes like two piss holes in the snow and driving home very cautiously,

Incidentally, Poulenc was gay. One way or the other.

OLD PAL

HE'D come sniffing around on our first day at the beach, an emaciated Anubis with his long pointed ears and snout, but we called him Pal after the tins of dogfood Miriam bought for him, together with a bowl. He'd filled out nicely in the last few days.

'You'd better say goodbye to him now,' Debbie said to her sister, combing water from her hair. I'd clean forgotten we were off again tomorrow. 'And we've still got all the packing to do.'

It sounded like hiccups as Miriam looked back at the beach where Pal was settling down for the night next to his bowl. He'd be waiting for us in the morning. I squeezed her hand and whispered, 'He'll be alright.'

OPEN WIDE

IT sounded bad enough from the waiting room as the dentist dug out Lisa's impacted molar piece by a tiny piece.

It was her first day out in years. If only people knew, looking at Lisa's children's book illustrations, so full of fun. What had gone wrong? Agoraphobia. For years now, there she sat, with never a breath of fresh air nor a touch of sun upon her face, just the pills and the vodka, enough to get her out to my car and to the dentist.

Back home, Lisa bawled through her butchered jaw, 'I want a drink.'

'You've had enough.' Tony, her boyfriend, hadn't worked in years either. They needed each other to yell at.

'Screw you!'

MEETING PLACE

MEMORY is fickle. So is time. Was this the same park bench we sat on however many years ago, she at one end, me at the other, miles apart? Our very last meeting. Nothing more to say.

So why had I asked for it? Because I couldn't let go, and that, as the Buddha said, was the cause of so much pointless grief.

'Hallo.' A tall, slim, mature, well-groomed, attractive female pointed to the bench. She smiled. 'May I?'

That was something else. The way good things always happen at the wrong time and place. What did the Buddha have to say about that?

I smiled back and stood up. 'All yours,' I said.

CAT FLAP

THE front door entry phone made me jump. A woman asked if she could leave a notice about a missing cat. Her name was Biscuit—the cat, not the woman.

Downstairs, I took her sad notice. 'Poor little Biscuit,' I said, but the woman had already gone, wrapped up and too cold to hang about under a sky as grey and hard as pumice.

It softened with clouds and rain, to trickle down all those other notices stuck on fences and round lampposts, of the same whiskery little face.

'Any luck?' Down at the shops, I thought I recognised the woman, much better in plastic mac and green wellies.

'Biscuit,' I added hopefully.

She hurried on, too wet to hang about.

WATCHING BRIEF

THERE'S no fool like an old fool, to which offence I stand as charged, waiting and watching by the window to catch sight of her on her way to work, waiting and watching each evening for her return.

The way she walks, the throwaway toss of her hair, the glimpse of her face, not conventionally pretty but with that cute little turned up nose, her clothes, even her shoes and my heart and soul are lost. It's something I've had to wait a lifetime to experience, now that it's far too late.

One thing might be said to help. Late autumn and the trees outside my window have shed their leaves, giving me a clearer view of the road. But then she's wrapped up in her winter scarf and coat.

I can't win. Does anybody?

TIBBET'S RIDE

FRAU Goering (as good a name as any), raincoat, woolly stockings and brogues, marched like a juggernaut, head and eyes locked straight ahead. An atom bomb up her arse would have made no difference. But she scared the shit out of me.

Most days she walked up the Hill as far as the Green Man and turned right by the Heath, leaving me at a safe distance behind to continue as far as Tibbet's Corner.

Mr Tibbet, highwayman and footpad, was said to have been hanged on that spot. Not true but it should have been, and that's how history is made. There's his monument amidst the circling traffic.

And there, coming towards me up Tibbet's Ride, was a figure in raincoat, woolly stockings, brogues and the plod of a fat Reichsmarschall.

Where was a gibbet when you needed one?

SOUTHERN BELLE

THE Mardi Gras was over and still February. In Jackson Square, a solitary black man blew a few tuneless notes on his battered sax and stopped to blow on his hands.

It was warmer on the bus. 'It's hot in here!' The voice, cracked and petulant, came from the back seats as we pulled out of the depot. Biloxi Mississippi, Mobile Alabama, Atlanta Georgia (coffee and donuts), Winston Salem North Carolina to the ceaseless whack of vulcanised rubber on road and the same cracked voice on and off for nigh on twenty hours.

At Washington DC, she squatted by the empty baggage hold, large wet snowflakes melting in her tangled iron-grey hair, sliding down her torn plastic mac. 'Where's my valise?' On A Streetcar Named Desire.

HEAVENS ABOVE

UNDER the anodyne white light of the crematorium chapel electronic music oozed out from somewhere and Mum's coffin moved slowly to the curtains at the back. She believed that when she died, she'd go straight into the arms of Jesus. The vicar had just said so too.

What about the Bible and the Creed and Christ coming back to summon us from our graves to be judged? And where would that leave Mum's small heap of ashes?

Back in the bright light of day, I shook the vicar's hand. What did he think? He'd been doing it for so long he probably didn't anymore. Let him get home to his tea.

And let my mum rest in the arms of Jesus or whatever.

NORTHERN LINE

THEY were doing A Midsummer Night's Dream in Regent's Park and Puck had jumped on our train with more mischief afoot.

How else to explain that single electrifying glance between me and the woman across the aisle as we rumbled through the tunnel? Warren Street, Goodge Street, and we dared not look again, nor hardly breathe. Charing Cross, Embankment.

Waterloo, and we both jumped up like we'd been stung. Waiting by the doors, if I'd reached out to touch her, we'd have blown every fuse from High Barnet to Morden.

Onto the platform, up the steps, along the corridor, onto the escalator. Please Puck, let her turn around. But he'd got off at Leicester Square.

Lord, what fools these mortals be!

EYEWITNESS

EDWARD had the hots for the Polish waitress. And with his soft transatlantic burr and those dark glasses, how could she resist?

A rhetorical question as we sat down to our working lunch to plan a new mail order project, The Great Composers. Yes, Tchaikovsky was gay and his marriage was a disaster. The dark glasses gave nothing away, but Edward knew a thing or two about marriage—or marriages. It was always some little thing, he said.

The Polish waitress handed us the wine list. Edward lowered the glasses to scan it and her. With one good eye and one that was black and blue.

Another of those little things, I supposed, as we settled for the Nuits Saint Georges.

DENTAL HEALTH

'YOU gotta laugh,' he said, same old flak jacket and the crutch of his jeans halfway down to his knees for his wedding tackle to swing in if he ever needed it.

He used to cross the road to avoid me. Now it was the other way round. 'Sometimes,' he said, 'I wanna top myself.' What he needed was a job. Start by stacking the shelves in Sainsbury's and move on from there. 'You're right,' he said, not for the first time, and it wouldn't be the last.

A fine drizzle settled on his tangled locks and on my packet of cornflakes. 'Still, you gotta laugh.' Through those two yellowed tombstones the dentists call incisors.

43

LAUGHING SAL

DIANA stared through the salt-caked windows of Cliff House to the hump of Seal Rock. Behind her a clutter of pinball games and miniature cranes dangled over tarnished trinkets and charms. The graveyard of a penny arcade.

But not quite dead. For a dime, a small mechanical organ or calliope, fed by a pair of wheezing bellows, blared out: 'The Stars and Stripes Forever'. Diana clapped her hands to her ears.

And Laughing Sal, a limbless torso in polka-dot smock, a wicked smile and a ginger wig. She shook and shuddered inside her glass case as she laughed and screamed. You could be drowning out there, grasping at the slippery sides of Seal Rock, while Sal just laughed and screamed. Hey, what fun?

FAG END

CYRIL was a head hunter's trophy, the grey shrunken face, the rictus of a grin, a few tufts of hair. And 40 fags a day for 40 years. Mind you, they'd kippered and cured him against all infection. As lively as a flea and as difficult to shake off.

'Hi there!' I squeezed in next to Anthea by the door. 'Good party!' Not with Cyril still around, fag on, and Anthea had gone.

Outside, I could at least breathe again. Onto a bus. Cyril hopped on behind me. He fiddled with his hearing aid. 'How far are you going?'

All the way with Anthea, given half a bleedin' chance.

IN MEMORIAM

A SHARP nip on my big toe, and out from under the sheet, a pair of little bright eyes and whiskers. Chocolate fur on top, snow-white underneath, he'd never seen a human before and I'd never been so close to a mouse. We regarded each other at leisure. Back on the floor, he poked his nose inside my half-packed bag, ready for the morning.

Stiff and tired after a day's travel, I reached in it for my keys and touched something furry and inert. Eyes now shut tight and tiny feet turned up in death, he'd left the pine-scented woods and sunflower fields for the gritty corner of my street.

God, rest his soul! And if he didn't have one, none of us did.

BABY FACE

'CAN you take Baby for a walk?' Beth pleaded as she mopped up in the car. She was into pet therapy, but five minutes with Baby and you'd be ready to jump off the Brooklyn Bridge.

At least things were quieter down Chestnut Street in sight of the Catskill Mountains. And quieter still in that empty gothic house staring back across an unweeded lawn.

But wait. Could I still hear the dark chime of a clock by the stairs, the creak of a floorboard up in the attic where the rocking horse tipped to and fro?

Baby had gone very quiet too, crouched by the side of the road. 'Come on, for God's sake.' I tugged at his lead before anyone else saw what we'd just done.

DELHI BELLY

MONSOON?' Geraldine scoffed. 'Rubbish.' All the same, with the roar of the rain, I could hardly think to play scrabble.

She won and wanted a drink. Scotch on the rocks for one.

'I'll swear it's nothing I gave you.' Cornflakes, toast and marmalade, a pot of tea. Florrie lit a new cigarette from the stub of the old, the last gasp of the raj as we watched the ambulance depart. She clapped her hands at a fat old crow perched by the window. They kept down the cockroaches, she said. This one took off with a dip of its wings and a bellyful of cockroach.

The aircraft dipped a wing over the fuzz of lights below.

'Drink sir?' A scotch and soda might help. 'Ice?'

'No thanks.'

CANDLELIGHT

PENNY tapped on my door just like Mimi in *La Boheme.* Both had a candle. Penny's flickered on top of my birthday cake.

I sometimes forgot what she looked and sounded like, until out in the street, on a bus or train, on the television, something another woman did or said brought her back like a thunder clap. She was there all the time, as Cole Porter wrote—Night and Day.

'Happy birthday!' she said. One candle to stand for too many more when it came to me and her. 'Aren't you going to blow it out?'

I did and it went dark, standing out there in the corridor. Penny took all that trouble to make me a lovely little cake but she wouldn't come in.

'Must rush.'

RAT RACE

IT'S not every day you see a rat meandering across the road of our busy High Street. Either he was old and had lost his wits or maybe he was drunk from a visit to the cellar of the Coach and Horses. Anyway, he'd gathered quite a crowd as he dodged the wheels of one vehicle and we cheered, missed the wheels of another and we cheered again. But not those of the bus.

And what about that fox with the hair on his tail almost gone, wandering past the station? He wasn't trying to cross the road. He knew when his time was up.

In the midst of life we are in death. Archbishop Cranmer, burnt at the stake.

TWO'S COMPANY

'MAY I?' With a silken kiss of her legs, she sat down across the table from me as the ship began to roll with the open sea. She raised her glass and smiled. 'Cheers!'

So what was she doing, on her own, on this ship, in the middle of the night? Trying to pick me up? She gazed out at the lights of the ferry going the other way. 'Ships that pass in the night,' she said dreamily.

'Hallo, darling.' She smiled again over my shoulder, at Bill. He had to take his pill and lie down. And there they were down on the car deck with the names Bill and Sandra stuck across their windscreen. Then we were off, in a blue-grey cloud of exhaust. Ships that pass in the night. And hangovers that don't.

BLUE NOTE

'ALL right,' Henry said as always. 'If you twist my arm.' I'd like to see Harriet or any of us try.

Henry was built like a heavyweight boxer, though he didn't play Rachmaninov with the gloves on. A useful guest at Harriet's dinner parties, he got up and padded over to her waiting baby grand. Brahms this time, the notes falling like autumn raindrops as she served coffee and handed round the chocolate mints.

He finished and glanced at his watch. Time to go. I drove him back to the station. 'Any more recitals coming up?' The ones he gave at this or that townhall.

Henry shook his head. His agent had just dropped him. A scholarship and three years at the Royal College of Music were not enough.

Even for a chocolate mint.

WATER SPORTS

MILLICENT screamed. She'd found a spider under a stone. 'A tarantula,' I told her. Not some giant but the real thing, named after the Italian town of Taranto, that also inspired a dance called the tarantella.

She just wanted to work on her tan, up there on the sun-baked hills. And not a spot of shade except for that old farmhouse. But wait. Next to it, wooden shutters opened upon a large cistern of crystal-clear water set into the hillside. What a place to sport like some mythic water sprite on such a day! Just don't let those shutters close on you again. Nowhere to cling to in the pitch dark, no one to hear you, alone up in those deserted hills.

Millicent, face now a lobster-red, kicked fretfully at her empty water bottle. I beckoned. 'Come over here and have a swim.'

LOST LADY

'EXCUSE ME.' She sat on a low garden wall, her voice as fragile as the rest of her. 'You see, I can't remember where I am.'

It could happen to any of us, so fragile is our own grasp on life. 'You don't recognise any of this?'

She shook her head and raised a thin, blue-veined hand against the sun. 'I say, Isn't that a lovely rose?'

White-tinged with crimson, a floral menstruation. 'Yes, and look at that bush of lavender, just in bloom.'

'How beautiful!'

'I love watching the bees buzzing and bobbing from branch to branch.'

She smiled. 'You must be a very happy man.'

I shook my head in turn. 'I'm too easily hurt.'

'Still, you've made me feel a whole lot better.'

I smiled back. 'Likewise.'

The trouble with conversations is remembering how they began.

65

BLACK COFFEE

EDITH said those flamboyant loops in my handwriting signified a wild imagination.

That wasn't all. She invited me to this big symposium on graphology. A long flight, a long, hot drive and a welcome break at Tonopah Joe's Truck Stop. Cinder-grey hills ringed the horizon, dust devils spun in the air and that heap of rocks, polished by a million years of sand and wind, giant coffee beans roasting under the noonday sun.

And Tonopah Joe? A dwarf in orange sweatshirt, tartan shorts and sneakers, a Nibelung of the Wild West, who crept out at night to chip away at those rocks.

Edith blew on the hot black brew in her cup. 'Good coffee,' she said.

'The best,' I agreed.

FACE OFF

'Cof gears, I raced off down the hill with Mr Hyde.
HRIST!' Beryl snatched the knife from me. 'I said,
cut off the head, not the bloody tail!'
I know, but I couldn't face that dead rheumy eye. Which end
did it matter anyway?

'Of course it matters!' Beryl had bought this large, wet
fish for her birthday party and it wouldn't quite fit in the oven.
'You bloody wimp!'

Her face was all twisted down one side. So was mine as I
glanced in my driving mirror. The way our faces could
suddenly change from good to bad.

Across the road, a baleful light shone behind Beryl's
kitchen curtains. 'Go back and make up before it's too late,'
said Dr Jekyll.

With a crunch

TOUCH TYPE

DEBBIE wasn't the touchy-feely type. She wouldn't even hold my hand when I so much wanted to hug her. 'The same with everybody,' she said.

Everybody? What about that fling with her boss? What about some of those other euphemistic boyfriends I'd picked up on? Oh, that was different.

I'll bet. With her kit off plenty of touchy-feely then, flesh upon flesh and every orifice up for grabs to the last coital grunt and gasp and a reach for the Kleenex.

'All in the past,' Debbie said. But all still there in memory.

All that pleasure without responsibility. Yes, and look who's talking.

SEA FEVER

DOWN on Ocean Beach, fugitive rainbows danced among the tumbling surf and the soles of my feet dug joyfully into the gleaming wet apron of the sea.

So what about those kids, prodding and kicking at something on the sand? The downward slit of the mouth, the cutlass-like tail fin, a young shark was stranded on the beach. Heavy, too, as I waded with him into the waves.

My good turn for the day except that a little while later he was back on the shore, too sick or too weak to swim against the tide.

Voracious predator he might have grown up to be, for the moment he was a fellow creature in distress. And the light went out of the day.

ANATOMY CLASS

A NNA sometimes poked the tip of her tongue out of the corner of her mouth, like a plump and juicy strawberry.

One of the few other parts of her I was ever likely to see. Breasts, so modestly withdrawn behind the cotton blouse with an expectant hint of nipple. Vulva and vagina, dressed perhaps with a neat little tuft of pubic hair, tucked away inside the jeans, and a little bit further round to that other orifice, its sphincter meant to expel but with a little digital persuasion willing and able to receive.

I'm sorry, Anna, if that's the direction my fevered mind is going. It's the only part of me that ever will. Please, just one lick at that strawberry before I die.

CHILLED OUT

WITH a gust of steam and Brussels sprouts, Adam burst out of the kitchen and out of the house, slamming the front door behind him.

Roberta and Adam, mother and son. Christmas made no difference. I drained my glass of sherry and bowed out with less commotion.

Plenty of merrymaking elsewhere, and in one brightly lit window, a large dining table abandoned to the dirty plates, nutshells, orange peel, spent crackers and streamers and old grandad fallen forward with his pink paper hat, fast asleep in his plum pudding and custard.

Someone else, hands in trouser pockets for warmth, joined me in contemplation of the scene.

I turned to Adam. 'Says it all, really.'

JOLLY ROGER

BANG. There was a skull and crossbones paper hat in Roger's cracker and a joke. Why did the tomato blush? Because it saw the salad dressing.

Wendy had invited me to the office Christmas party but enough was enough. Never mind the rain. I stepped out to the Emperor Concerto. Musical nicknames—Moonlight Sonata, Raindrop Prelude. My next little piece for *In Classical Mood*.

In the old days, I'd have it on Roger's desk before he could say Dmitri Shostakovich. Not since Wendy had arrived as his temp. His personal assistant now and you needed a bloody passport to see him.

A taxi pulled up at the lights. Was that her inside, with a skull and crossbones, somewhat askew? The lights turned green.

Next stop, Wapping, Execution Dock, where they hanged the likes of him.

MIDDLE C

'SIT up straight,' I said, pressing gently into the small of her back. 'Opposite note Middle C, hands well above the keyboard.' Rosemary wanted to play the piano.

Let's start with the scale of C major, all on the white notes of the keyboard. 'Slowly does it. Thumb under on note F in the right hand or you'll run out of fingers.'

I guided hers with mine in a sweet little *pas de deux*. As close as I'd ever get with Rosemary. Not like those boyfriends, you can bet.

'Now try the left hand.' Her fingers so soft and white as they touched the keyboard. Touched, felt, stroked, held, caressed, fondled, clutched.

Towards a different Middle C.

LAST RITES

IF getting stuck in someone else's funeral cortege wasn't bad enough, it was pissing down and we were lost. Still trapped between two big black limousines, we watched them return to the home of the deceased. 'Come on,' I said to Jill, 'they owe us one, and with that crowd they'll never notice us.'

Cognac, Armagnac, it hit the spot. 'They should do a Michelin Guide to some of these cemeteries, crosses for interest, skulls for atmosphere.'

A decent claret too. 'The funeral baked meats did coldly furnish forth the marriage table.' I smacked my lips. 'Hamlet.'

'Alas! Poor Yorick.' Jill waved her glass.

I handed her a fork. 'Better eat something.'

'A funeral baked bean?' She collapsed with laughter and a bowl of mayonnaise.

'I think,' she said, 'I'm going to be sick.'

SPIDERMAN

'LOOK at a pianist's fingers, like the legs of a giant spider as they run up and down the keyboard.' A spider with a limp in my case.

Her own hands and fingers neatly clasped on her lap, Cindy had asked me to play something. 'Nothing like live music,' she said. It was music that brought us together. I liked to think there was a bit more to it than that. Self-deception is a sad and pitiful thing.

Cindy shook out her long, dark hair. Still not a single thread of grey to be seen. White in my case, what I had left of it.

She smiled. 'You do say some funny things sometimes.'

Yes, to stop me from crying.

STILL LIFE

IT went back to those swollen blue-veined breasts when I finally got Carol into bed. A total turn-off. Driving her down to my little house in France, was saying sorry.

Her face still flushed from last night's wine, the line of dark grey hills marking the horizon seemed never to get any closer as we speeded along mile after mile. Till suddenly at a turn of the road they did, drawing apart like curtains upon a stage to reveal our first vineyard, the rows of vines immaculately staked out on the hillside, young green shoots calling down the sun. Carol sat up.

Another turn in the road and I swerved to avoid the mangled body of a fox or hare. She buried her face in her hands.

First it was boobs. Now this.

TITBITS

'IT'S the subconscious,' I said. 'You can flog your guts out on a piece of work, sleep on it and next morning, your subconscious has done it all for you, word for word.'

Sue was a good listener. She needed to be with me around and hardly ever a word to say for herself. Till the day she shut me up with those pen and ink drawings, more powerful than any words, abstract patterns filled with what I can only describe as deep turmoil and passion.

'My God, Sue, you play your cards so close to your chest and all the time look what you've been hiding behind those boobs.' Good and firm they were beneath the woollen jumper, filled with all that passion.

And enough to make her blush.

HALF CUT

'CAN you take over for a minute?' By my alley Julian, in vest and pants, was down on his hands and knees with a pair of scissors.

His girlfriend, Yvonne, had gone away for the weekend and asked him to feed her prize Burmese cat Mistinguett. When the latter started her caterwauling, he chucked her out. Come Monday morning, he was creeping round the village trying to lure her back with that sound Yvonne made as she cut up slices of fish for Mistinguett.

To see him now you'd never guess that Julian's paintings sold for megabucks in London, Paris and New York. Would he give me one if I found Mistinguett? I turned the corner.

'All right, go fuck yourself!' Snip snip.

SUNDAY BREAK

BETH needed to do her number twos. The nurse helped her to the toilet but, oh dear, not quite fast enough. First, my wife and then more like a sister. She was dying and we both knew it.

And such a beautiful summer's day outside. Alice was out there somewhere, with whom I didn't know, and probably just as well.

On the tube train rumbling through the dark to the peristaltic wobble of pipes along the tunnel wall, I took comfort from the few other passengers, a poultice against my woes.

Back on my bed, a soft rippling light came from the trees outside my window, alive with sunlight. And Alice was out there somewhere.

CANINE CRUNCH

'POOR darling,' Pat said. 'It's the heat.' Yappy Popeyes was a bug-eyed beetle or a chihuahua, a breed of dog from Mexico, where one of those hats would have snuffed him out. He'd just thrown up.

Yes, but pleasantly cool in Corinne's garden, in the shade. Her old cat ambled in looking for a spot of it. Yappy Popeyes let out a half-strangled howl. 'Get rid of that cat!' Pat cried.

Never mind her. From the house came a crash. Caliban had broken loose again. God knows what sort of dog he was but he now burst into the garden, all shaggy hair and dribble. He made straight for Pat. I wonder why.

LATIN LESSON

THE sun hit us like a fist as we stepped out of the church. Across the dry, scorched fields, old and dying almond trees, black, cracked and broken looked crucified beneath it.

'By the way,' I said to Priscilla, 'the letters INRI over that crucifix stand for *Iesus Nazarenus Rex Iudaeorum*, Jesus of Nazareth King of the Jews. There wasn't a letter J in the Latin alphabet.'

I took a breath. 'Here's another one, SPQR, the proud legend of the Roman legions. *Senatus Populusque Romanus*, The senate and people of Rome. The que was the Latin for 'and'.

Through her sunglasses, Priscilla watched a buzzard, wings outstretched, circling lazily on a thermal high in the hot, deep blue dome of the sky. 'Thank you, Mr Clever Clogs.'

'Anytime.'

BEDTIME STORY

THE programme was about black holes, the void where a star had once been, with a gravitational force so strong that even light couldn't escape from it. In other words, black.

I switched the television off at last. The sleeping pills were kicking in and I couldn't escape forever. Me and Emily. Friendship, if it has any real foundation, takes years of affection and trust to build. The quiet knowing little smiles and private jokes. Why bring the madness of love into it, push it till it breaks? Years to build, moments to destroy.

'Why can't we still be friends?' Emily had pleaded. The face had faded, but not the voice. In the middle of the night.

NIGHT WATCH

A S I climbed the stairs on my return, there was a faint smell of death in the air. Dead wasps lay on the floor. Others wandered up and down the window pane. They'd dropped into the bedroom from their nest on the roof.

I'd always quite liked wasps, with their gaily striped black and yellow bodies, long, slender wings, little nodding heads and a taste for jam, and they didn't sting if you left them alone.

A point to reflect upon as I lay prostrate upon my bed through the long, sleepless night, nauseous and feverish, pulse racing madly from all those stings. Trying to shove a piece of paper into the gap in the ceiling wasn't leaving them alone.

Night and day, they never slept. Rustling, nibbling away up there. The tinnitus of the damned.

DINNER DATE

SEATED at the baby grand in a corner of the dining hall, shutters and windows open to the boom of surf at midday, to the blood-red sun spilling into a dead calm sea, I watched her watching me across the floor.

I'd seen her down by the pool, reading a book, quite happy to be on her own, hair turning grey but a body that still had something to give. Now in a silvery dress that sparkled each time she moved and hair brushed back over her ears, one of a jolly dinner party but watching me watching her across the floor.

The last chord of Gershwin's *Embraceable You* and they all got up to go, laughing, chatting, with a scraping of chairs. And with one last glance over her lightly tanned shoulder for us both to remember.

BEASTLY BUSINESS

SINCE I was in Ward 66, I became the Beast 666.

I'd collapsed, rolled off the bed and couldn't get up again. Somehow, Frances had got me into a chair, called an ambulance and off I went.

Ward 66 and a spell in Intensive Care, a cavernous place of dim but perpetual light and what looked like mummies wrapped in white being moved about. Hades.

What I hated was the oxygen mask that made a noise like someone being garrotted. Why any noise when oxygen was a gas? Why lots of things till they let me go home again?

Frances was waiting. She loved me because I got her name right. I just loved and adored her. The beast with Zimmer frame.

MONKEY BUSINESS

ON the bus taking us to the ruined temple with the sacred monkeys, she kept tossing back her raven-black locks to sneak another glance at the mystery man behind his silver-tinted dark glasses. You can tell.

On arrival, I took them off to treat her to a smile. A simian hand snatched them from me. A sacred sphincter disappeared behind some rocks.

'Talk about cheeky monkey!' she bawled, for everyone else from the bus to hear. Desperately, I turned and bought another pair of sunglasses to hide behind. A plastic eyepiece fell straight out.

'Be seein' yer, Lord Nelson!'

FLYING HIGH

ONE swallow doesn't make a summer, like the one now diving, twisting against the backdrop of an inky sodden sky.

Time was when you were suddenly aware of their joyous little screams and knew that summer had arrived. They'd flown thousands of miles over blazing desert, over sea and yet more land to get here, many of them falling by the wayside and more doomed to perish going back again.

Perhaps not so joyous after all. Survival of the fittest in the grim face of nature. That said, they're a rare-enough presence these days. What's happened? Climate change? And are they bound for extinction?

The first raindrops splashed against my window. Don't get wet, my solitary little friend.

CURTAIN CALL

TONY'S Canon Chasuble elbowed his way to the bar, digging Peter's Algernon sharply in the ribs. Jeremy, the director and Peter's best friend, clenched his fists. He played rugby too. Julia adjusted her wig and squeezed my hand. 'See you round the carpark.'

The smiling curtain calls, and all the bitchiness behind them, perhaps worse among amateurs who felt they'd forfeited their true vocation. Coming up the path behind me, someone in dog collar and gaiters tripped and fell. Peter giggled. Jeremy emerged from the shadows. Julia tugged at her seatbelt. 'Let's go.'

Past that church flying the flag. 'St George for England! St Pancras for Scotland!' A good old chestnut for Tony in the Tudor Players' Christmas pantomime.

If he still had his teeth.

RED ALERT

HERPES Zoster isn't the name of some ancient fire god, it's shingles, though the pain is like being burnt alive. 'Oh, you poor boy!' Rosalind said when I delivered my copy. 'You should be in bed.' I know, but she wasn't there to tuck me in.

The angry buzz by her phone announced that Toby, her boss, had first call. He bawled at her all day, then once a week took her out to dinner and the hotel afterwards. Otherwise, stuck at home with her invalid mother. What else was there?

Back at her desk, Rosalind made a big thing of blowing her nose. 'We're a fine pair, aren't we?'

Yes, and why couldn't we have had a go. At least I'd still be there when she woke up.

DOG DAYS

THEY call it *'la canicule'* or 'little dog', a heatwave that comes with the appearance of Cirius, the dog star. In other words, the dog days, when canines pant and scratch their fleas.

Not the Pekinese at the restaurant. He just whined and whimpered. Nor was it the heat, but another dog under the next table. It took a lot to rouse him, but the whining and whimpering did it in the end. He yanked himself to his feet, toppling the table with a crash of cutlery, plates and glasses.

It nearly ended in a fight, and not between the dogs.

So much for a romantic evening under the stars. That very bright one might be Cirius. Closer to hand, the hot, dry hills withdrew into the night.

CELTIC FRINGE

'SHAME about the parade.' Through the window, a blurred city skyline was dotted with those rooftop water tanks, urban beehives collecting the grimy, wet pollen of the streets. St Patrick's Day in the rain.

'Ah!' Eamon, our janitor, added a drop of the hard stuff to our cups of coffee. 'Never mind. Here's to Brian Boru, the great king of old Ireland, and his harp that you'll see on every good bottle of Guinness!'

We took another drop of the hard stuff and Eamon began to sing, 'If you ever go across the sea to Ireland.' Unless it was 'Danny Boy'.

Going back down the stairs seemed a lot harder than coming up them. Three flights down to the elevator. Out of order.

I knew there was something.

EN VACANCES

SWIFTS and swallows crowned the brightest day with little shrieks of joy as we drove through Pont Saint Esprit. Bridge of the Holy Spirit.

Dora clapped her hands. 'What a lovely name, dear!' Reg swiped at a fly.

Auntie Dora and Uncle Reg who used to send me socks for Christmas. I hardly remembered them, but Dora hadn't forgotten me. Now on their coach tour, with half a day to spare, they'd dug me out. I'd better take them somewhere.

'Take your cap off, dear.' In the gloom of the chapel painted columns rose to a vaulted ceiling of midnight-blue patterned with stars. Dora took my hand. 'It's all so lovely. Reg doesn't say much, but I know he's loving it too.'

Back in the car, nose starting to peel, Reg swiped at a fly.

NEEDLEWORK

WHY should I have to step into the road to avoid someone else's garbage? Because that's what it was.

Prince Albert had a lot to answer for with his Christmas trees. The lovely little conifers planted in their tens of thousands, to be uprooted, castrated, trussed up, ready for sale. A few days in some hot, stuffy room, dressed with fairy lights and trinkets, and when the fun was over, chucked into the street for someone else to deal with.

With my shoe, I began to shift the corpse of this one into the road between two parked cars, leaving behind a trail of dead needles, its trail of blood. A faint scent of resin hung in the air, of pinewoods and dappled sunlight. Even in death, it tried to please.

SMOKE SIGNALS

THAT boulder by the corner of the Rue de l'Horloge must be a meteorite, of an unimaginable weight, and shiny black from the polish of her backside on sunny days.

My neighbour, the face of a wrinkled walnut, woolly stockings and clogs. The creak and groan of her shutter at break of day, the creak and groan at eventide, and in between the rancid smoke from her chimney as she burnt her ordures.

Except when I returned last spring to find the boulder was an empty throne, no creak and groan to wake me, no more smoke from those ordures.

In the cemetery, I searched in vain for a grave, while that chimney stood sooty black against a radiant evening sky. Spontaneous combustion. What else?

BOTTOMS UP

A HINT of *creme de menthe*, I thought, in Jim's concoction. He repaired computers but was also writing a book on cocktails.

I grabbed his phone. 'Fiona?' My editor, the county set, neurotic, snappy, with a face and hands like that painting, 'The Scream'.

'Listen Fiona good news. My computer's up and running again. And something else right up your street. Jim here is writing a book on cocktails. You know, Manhattan, Bloody Mary, Brass Monkey, Zombie, Screwdriver, Rusty Nail, Sex on the Beach, Between the Sheets, Strip and Go Naked, Harvey Wallbanger. What? Wall Fiona, as in bricks. Banger as in sausage.'

The stupid bitch hung up. I held out my glass and pointed to Jim's silver shaker. 'Any more of that stuff?'

POSTSCRIPT

I F you're in a hole, stop digging. Like all good advice, hard to take on board. I crossed another word out here, added another one there, as though that did any good.

Outside my window, the still tender and unsullied leaves shivered in the wind, and down the road was that abandoned car with all the parking tickets stuck to the windscreen and on the dashboard that little striped tiger, button eyes raised hopelessly to the world. That's why I had to go the long way round to the shops. Couldn't face them.

Mind you, there might be a nice little story there. A new hole to start digging when I got back from the shops. Bread, soup, fish fingers.

Printed in the USA
CPSIA information can be obtained
at www.ICGtesting.com
LVHW021834230823
755929LV00016B/690